Raintree is an imprint of Capstone Global Library Limited,
a company incorporated in England and Wales having its
registered office at 264 Banbury Road, Oxford, OX2 7DY –
Registered company number: 6695582

www.raintree.co.uk
myorders@raintree.co.uk

Text © Capstone Global Library Limited 2019
The moral rights of the proprietor have been
asserted.

Designed by Bob Lentz
Original illustrations © Capstone Global Library
Limited 2019
Production by Kris Wilfahrt
Originated by Capstone Global Library Ltd
Printed and bound in India

ISBN 978 1 4747 5179 7
22 21 20 19 18
10 9 8 7 6 5 4 3 2 1

British Library Cataloguing in
Publication Data
A full catalogue record for this book is
available from the British Library.

by Matthew K. Manning

illustrated by Joey Ellis

THE
SEARCH
FOR
STALOR

raintree

a Capstone company — publishers for children

LEGEND SAYS . . .

The Rainbow-Barfing Unicorns
come from a faraway, magical
world called Pegasia. Not so
long ago, these stinky, zombie-
like, vomiting creatures were
banished to Earth for being, well
. . . stinky, zombie-like, vomitng
creatures. However, Earth presents
them with a new danger: humans.

So, just who are the Rainbow-Barfing
Unicorns . . . ?

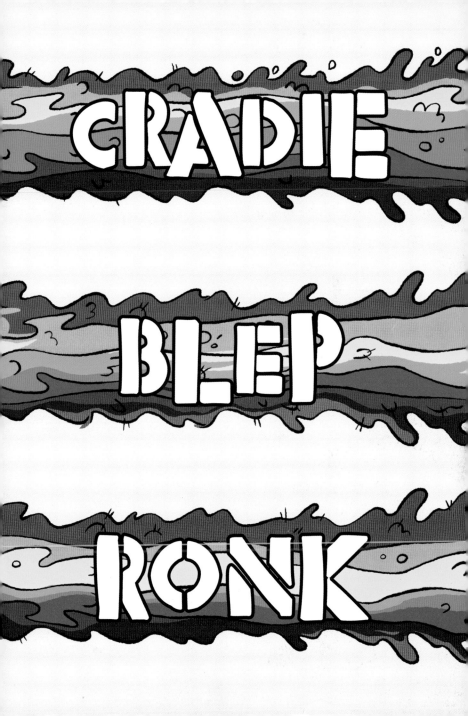

CHAPTER ONE

The sun was shining on the Brown Sugar Fields. But then again, the sun seemed to always shine in Pegasia. Its gentle rays caught the candied grass in the perfect warm glow, like a technician staging the lighting on a film set.

If one of the unicorns that populated this mystical world happened to stand in a sunbeam, he or she would most certainly notice the faint odour of caramel or lemon, depending on the sun's mood that day.

On this particular afternoon, the sun was outdoing itself. It was the perfect weather for a frolic in the fields. Or in this case, a game of the much-sung-about hoofball.

Grape Sorbet wasn't paying attention to the game, however. While she was doing her best to hide it, she couldn't help staring at Stalor. He was on the other team, but that didn't matter to Grape. She'd kick the hoofball, then look for Stalor's reaction.

Usually, he wasn't watching her. He'd be running towards the ball, galloping through the field with his brilliant mane floating in the cherry-scented breeze. Every so often, his large hooves would crash down on a candy cane weed sticking out of the ground.

Every so often, he would kick up the sweet, powdery, chocolate-flavoured dirt in his hurry. But every so often, he would steal a glance back at Grape Sorbet and smile.

Stalor's perfect teeth were a true gift worth looking in a horse's mouth, even if that wasn't quite the saying. Grape swore that the light gleamed off his smile each time he'd grin. She'd even hear a *bling* sound in her head, as if he were a handsome cartoon character. It was all she could do not to get weak in her purple knees, all four of them.

"You playin' or what?" said the annoyed voice of Raspberry Jelly from behind her.

Grape turned to see her friend and teammate. He passed the ball to her, making a disapproving grunting noise. Raspberry always disapproved of something. Usually, that something was Stalor.

With a smile on her face, Grape dribbled the ball between her hooves. She had a knack for hoofball. She just didn't usually let people see her skills.

She sped past Tapioca Pudding, which in and of itself wasn't too hard to do. Tapioca rarely concentrated on much of anything, even hoofball. At the moment he was busy munching on a piece of peppermint bark that he had discovered near the halfway line.

"Pudding!" Stalor called at his teammate. Tapioca ignored the scolding and took another bite of his bark.

Stalor galloped towards Grape Sorbet as Grape neared the pair of chocolate orange trees that were serving as their goal posts. Unfortunately for her, Grape made the mistake of looking at the handsome unicorn hurrying her way.

She blushed when she caught a glimpse of
his dark, mysterious blue eyes. Then she
promptly tripped over the ball.

Stalor didn't hesitate. He
kicked the ball away from
Grape Sorbet's fallen
purple body and stormed
down the pitch towards
the hole in the rock
candy formation that
the unicorns used as the
opposing goal.

Raspberry sped towards
Stalor. But just as he gained on
him, a shadow fell across the pitch.
All four unicorns looked up at the same time.
There was something plummeting towards them.
And it was very, very large.

"Pickles! A tonne of pickles!" Stalor yelled.

"What?" said Grape in a confused voice. Stalor wasn't making sense. A tonne of pickles was certainly not heading their way. It looked almost like . . . a meteorite.

"Pickles! And they are gre-e-een!" Stalor screamed again.

Then the meteorite hit. And everything else went green.

CHAPTER TWO

Cradie woke up in a cold sweat. She looked around her stable. Ronk and Blep were sleeping soundly in their corners. Each had his head down on his mattress, and his eyes closed shut. Ronk was sleeping on his back with his hooves straight up in the air. Cradie would have been concerned had her odd companion not slept that way every night since they'd arrived on Earth.

Ronk had been a bit off even before that day in the Brown Sugar Fields when the meteorite

had struck. But breathing in the green gas that
seeped out of the fallen chunk of space rock
certainly didn't help matters.

Ronk had stopped being Tapioca Pudding on
that afternoon. The stuff in the gas – the "zombie
virus" for lack of a better term – had changed
his white coat to green. It had caused his eyes to
glow a sickly yellow colour, his skin to crack and
flake off at every opportunity. It had cost Tapioca

Pudding many of his teeth, and the ones that remained, well, they certainly weren't anything to look at with their many stains and cracks.

But worst of all, the green gas had caused Tapioca to lose his voice. Now, instead of telling cheesy jokes or complaining that he was hungry (which was always), Pudding could only say his new name. He could only say, "RONK!"

Blep wasn't much better off. His bright red coat had faded, as if he'd been left out in a shop window for decades. He was a bit off-putting to look at, too. That wasn't an issue for Cradie. She was used to his purple mane, his dry skin and even his fungus-covered hooves. But to a normal unicorn, to the average citizen of Pegasia, Blep was a freak of nature. He was certainly no longer Raspberry Jelly. He was just Blep, a sarcastic unicorn who now looked as salty as he behaved.

Cradie had got used to her two friends now that they had been banished to Earth. But she still wasn't quite used to her own zombie body. It didn't seem fair. You try to eat one unicorn's delicious-smelling hoof, and they kick you out of your world completely.

Just because she and her friends had developed an uncontrollable taste for sweets, and wanted to devour her unicorn pals whenever they got close to her, she was sent through a portal to this dimension. To make matters worse, while she still craved sweets, if she ate any, she was forced to instantly barf a perfect rainbow out of her mouth and into the sky.

It didn't make sense.

But not much had made sense since the day Grape Sorbet transformed into the pale, scratchy unicorn they call Cradie.

"Hmph," Cradie said.

That would be enough feeling sorry for herself for one day. Life was pretty good here on Earth, all things considered. They had their human friend Xander looking out for them. He was the one that arranged for them to have a home at the Montgomery Apple Orchard and Farm.

While only twelve years old, Xander had come up with the idea of having the zombie unicorns wear thick make-up and more than a little air-freshener spray in order to star in a stage show: Xander and the Rainbow-Barfing Unicorns. It was a big hit in this small mountain town. And when Cradie barfed a rainbow in front of a crowd, they assumed it was just the big final number in the act. The audience thought they were witnessing a magic trick, not real, actual magic.

Of course the best thing about living at the

orchard was the establishment next door: the Henderson Landfill.

Cradie stood up and stretched her faded purple legs. She shook her mane. It didn't move much. It was matted down to her coat from sleeping on it wrong and from whatever gross gunk had got stuck in it during the night. Cradie seemed to attract all types of weird stuff ever since she had become a sweet-obsessed zombie.

She walked out of the stable door and through the grass. Then she pulled open the back gate to the rubbish dump and walked inside. There she saw a fresh pile of bin bags that had been dropped off the day before. It would be as good a midnight snack as any.

The bright moon shone down on her as she took a bite of a black plastic bag, revealing a dirty yoghurt container and an apple core.

Cradie chewed on them slowly. Rubbish was easy on her stomach. She didn't barf a single rainbow as she ate the entire contents of the bin bag.

When she had finished, she turned around to leave. She felt sleepy again. It was still a good six hours before daybreak.

"Did you have another dream?" Blep said. He was standing behind her.

She wasn't sure how long he had been there. Blep could be quiet when he wanted to be. It wasn't often. But he could do it.

"Yeah," Cradie answered.

She looked down at the ground. She knew how Blep felt about Stalor. He'd always seemed to hate that particular unicorn. Maybe it was jealousy. Stalor was known as the most handsome unicorn in Pegasia. And everyone in Pegasia was attractive to start with.

Even after the virus, Stalor still retained his colouring. Only his eyes gave him away as a zombie. They were a sickly yellow-green now. But Cradie was sure she could still get lost in them.

Blep didn't share that opinion, for whatever reason.

"Huh," said Blep. "So a nightmare?"

"Yeah, but it didn't make much sense," said Cradie. "Stalor was in it, and he kept talking about pickles."

"That explains the midnight snack, I suppose."

"Ha!" Cradie laughed a quiet laugh. "Maybe."

"All right then," said Blep. "It's settled."

Cradie was confused. "What? What are we talking about?"

"We've been here long enough without your buddy," said Blep. "Let's go and find him."

"Stalor?"

"That's right," said Blep. He turned to walk towards their stable.

"You want to find Stalor?"

"No," said Blep. "But I'll help you find him anyway."

"But we have no idea where to look," said Cradie. "Or we would have found him by now."

"So we'll keeping looking until he turns up," said Blep. "Simple as that."

Cradie stood still as Blep walked out of the dump. She would have run over and hugged her friend, if she thought Blep knew how. But instead, she trotted back to the stable to help wake up Ronk.

CHAPTER THREE

"So OK," said Blep. "Let's go over what we know."

Cradie and the still-rather-sleepy Ronk stood in front of Blep inside their stable. Blep had switched on a torch. It shone upwards towards the wooden ceiling. The eerie glow from the light made a tiny circle on the rafters, spotlighting a bird's nest and a sparrow that would have much rather been sleeping at that moment.

"When we got shoved through that portal by our . . . let's say by our former friends," said Blep. "When that happened, we lost your pal Stalor."

Cradie gave Blep a reprimanding look. "*Our* pal Stalor," she corrected.

"Yeah, yeah," said Blep. "Sure."

"RONK," Ronk said. It didn't add much to the conversation, so Blep continued.

"So did anyone see Stalor actually go through the portal?" asked Blep. "Like, is there a chance the guy's still in Pegasia?"

"No," said Cradie. "He went through. He was last, but I know I saw him. I looked backwards right as I fell into that weird swirling light. He was there behind me."

"But there was no sign of him when we reappeared here on Earth, on that mountain behind Xander's house," said Blep.

26

"RONK," said Ronk. He nodded his head. The torch flickered. It seemed to be as low on batteries as Ronk was low on brainpower.

"So what happened?" said Blep. "Did he just arrive later than us? Could he be wandering around Xander's mountain right now? Or could he have touched down somewhere else?"

"That's what I don't understand," said Cradie. "He was behind us, and then he wasn't."

The torch flickered again. Ronk looked at it, and then walked to the corner of the room. He picked up a small twig that had somehow got mixed in with the straw that lined the stable's floor. He brought it back to his friends, but when he placed it down on the ground in front of Cradie, the torch beam died completely.

"RONK," Ronk said in an annoyed tone.

Then once again he was moving slowly across

the room. He got to his mattress and nudged his nose underneath. He couldn't see anything due to the darkness, but his nose was still working fine. Or as fine as anything of Ronk's worked.

He found what he was sniffing for, and popped his head back out from under his mildewing bed. Then he walked back to Cradie and Blep.

"Ronk?" asked Cradie, sounding remarkably like her strange friend.

"RONK," Ronk answered. He was quite sure of himself. Then he swallowed the thing he had been hiding under his mattress. It was a half-eaten chocolate bar. He had been saving it for an important occasion.

Less than a minute later, Ronk pointed his head towards the ceiling.

"RONK!"

He barfed a blindingly brilliant rainbow.

Now able to see once again, Blep and Cradie looked down at the twig in front of Ronk. With the light of the rainbow still hanging in the air of the stable, they could see the stick quite clearly. It was a normal twig, but one that branched out in two different ways at its centre.

"Are you . . . ," Cradie began. "Are you saying that the portal we took here . . . That it branched out in two different directions? Like it had a fork in the road?"

"RONK," Ronk said. He nodded his head.

"And you saw this? With your own eyes?" Cradie asked.

"**RONK,**" Ronk said again. He was still nodding.

"So he wasn't sent to the mountain at all," said Blep. "Stalor went somewhere completely different. He might not even be in the same dimension as us."

"**RONK,**" Ronk said for the third time.

At that, the Rainbow-Barfing Unicorns went quiet. The rainbow light faded, and the room fell back into darkness.

CHAPTER FOUR

"For the crime of attempted unicorn eating, I hereby declare you banished," said Mayor Blueberry Strudel.

It was obvious that the decision hurt Blueberry's feelings. Banishment from Pegasia was almost never done. The pain of punishing his fellow unicorns was all over his face.

Deputy Mayor Sprinkle Shortbread III read her colleague's expression and decided to chime in. She was only a week away from becoming Pegasia's new mayor, after all. It was high time she took her responsibilities seriously.

"You may step through the portal now," said Shortbread. "Never to return."

"I think we should talk about this," Grape Sorbet wanted to say. But instead, her words came out as a hungry growl, *"Rruuuuhhhh!"*

Mayor Strudel was about to respond, but that's when Tapioca Pudding lunged at him. He was gnashing his teeth, attempting to take a rather large bite out of the mayor's backside.

"RONK!" he yelled.

Deputy Mayor Shortbread was too quick for him, however. She leaped forward and used her head to butt Ronk through the swirling magic portal in front of them.

"*Ronnnnnnnnn—*" Ronk began, but his voice trailed off until there was nothing left.

Without arguing, Raspberry Jelly stepped through after his friend. His face looked defeated and angry. Raspberry's angry expression was familiar to Grape Sorbet. The defeated look was not. But soon, Grape couldn't see him at all, as the portal seemingly gobbled him up.

"*Rruuuuhhhh!*" Grape grunted again.

It wasn't what she wanted to say at all. But the zombie virus was strong inside her. She couldn't seem to get a word out as long as she was near her other unicorn friends. Her other delicious-looking friends.

Grape turned and leaped through the portal in a huff. As she fell through the swirling mass of light, she could hear Stalor behind her.

"Not me," he was saying. "Take them, fine. But . . . rrrruu . . . not me. I'm not sick . . . I'm not–"

Grape Sorbet turned around and watched as Stalor fell through the brightly lit air. Someone must have shoved him inside the portal. His face certainly looked surprised.

"We're – we're in quite the pickle!" he shouted.

"Again with the pickles?" Grape found herself saying.

"A tonne of pickles!" Stalor yelled.

Grape turned away from him. She was tired of hearing about pickles and wanted to see where she was going to land. In the far distance, she could see a small, circular opening. It looked as if there was grass beyond it. Perhaps there were trees, too.

She braced herself for impact, but all she could hear was Stalor yelling behind her.

"A whole tonne of pickles!" he yelled. "They're gre-eee-eeeeeen!" He screamed that last part again and again and again.

CHAPTER FIVE

"A whole tonne of pickles!" Cradie declared as she woke up.

"A whole what now?" Blep said.

Cradie looked around the stable. Early morning light was seeping in through the slats in the wooden walls.

"Pickles?" Cradie said. She seemed confused. She was starting to get her bearings now.

She and the other Rainbow-Barfing Unicorns had fallen back asleep after the light of the rainbow had gone out. Things had seemed so hopeless last night.

But now, everything was different. She was filled with a happiness she hadn't felt since they arrived on Earth. It was as if she had found a puzzle piece that had been lost under a sofa cushion for years. She just didn't know what puzzle it fit into quite yet.

"No pickles for you," said Xander as he opened the stable door. The cool morning air filled the room and gave Cradie a quick shiver. "I don't want you barfing any rainbows until this afternoon's performance."

"A tonne of pickles," Cradie said to herself. She was talking in a quiet voice, so it was easy for Xander to mishear her.

"Pickletown?" he said. "It's not really a town
of pickles, you know."

"What are we talking about?" asked Blep.
He had got to his hooves and was walking over to
greet Xander.

Xander patted his shaggy mane.

"I'm not sure," said Xander. "How did you even hear about Pickletown?" he asked Cradie.

"What is a Pickletown?" she said.

"You brought it up," said Xander.

"No," said Cradie. "I said a *tonne* of pickles."

"Who did what in the where now?" asked Blep. He was still confused.

"RONK?" Ronk said as he walked over towards Cradie. He seemed even more confused than the others.

"Wait," said Cradie. "There's a place called Pickletown? Like a real city around here?"

"Well, yeah," said Xander. "I mean Pickletown is just its nickname. It's really called Littleton. But there was a pickle factory there for decades, and the name sort of–"

"We need to go there right now!" interrupted Cradie. "Right now, Xander!"

Xander would probably have asked a few follow up questions, but he didn't get the chance. Cradie had already shot out of the stable and was halfway to the car park. So he and the rest of the Rainbow-Barfing Unicorns had no other choice but to follow her.

CHAPTER SIX

"Can't this thing go any faster?" Cradie yelled from the trailer behind Xander's bicycle.

"Huff . . . huff," Xander said in reply.

"I think that's a yes," said Blep. "If there weren't three of us in here."

Xander turned to look back at Blep. Xander was too winded to speak, but he could manage a nod.

"See?" said Blep. He tucked his head back underneath the blanket Xander had used to cover them.

While it wasn't the best way to disguise the unicorns, it certainly didn't hurt to have them mostly obscured when riding in his trailer. Cradie didn't do the same, however. Some part of her thought that if she kept her eyes on the road, they'd get to Pickletown faster. It wasn't the cleverest part of her.

The bike did seem to be having a tough go of it. Xander was nearing the top of a hill. He had to stand up now in order to press down on his pedals hard enough just to not roll backwards.

"So . . . huff . . . ," Xander began. "You . . . you had . . . huff . . . a dream about . . . Pickletown?"

"Sort of," said Cradie. "I just know we have to go there."

"Huff," Xander answered.

"RONK!" Ronk said from beneath the blanket. No one really seemed to pay attention to him.

At the top of the hill, the country road changed to a city street. Or at least it was what passed for a city street in a small little place like Pickletown. Cradie let out something between a gasp and a sigh of relief as Xander steered them under an arching sign that read: Welcome to Littleton – America's "Pickletown".

Xander saw a bike rack on the pavement. It was the perfect excuse for him to stop pedalling and get a breather. He pulled into it. Then he hopped off and chained up his bike. Cradie watched from the trailer, her body half covered by Xander's blanket. Beside her, two lumps fidgeted. They moved as if restless inside their hiding spot.

While Cradie had put up quite a protest, Xander had managed to douse the unicorns in make-up before they left the orchard. The job had been rushed. Xander could see some of Cradie's powder rubbing off onto the blanket. But it would do for now. The Rainbow-Barfing Unicorns needed to look like they were wearing fake horns and were simply painted in bizarre colours. It wouldn't be a good thing if people realized the unicorns were the real deal. Xander was fortunate in the fact that most people don't believe in unicorns, let alone expect to see them walking the streets of a place called Pickletown.

He headed over to his trailer. Xander picked up the pace a little after seeing the anxiety in Cradie's face. He was still mostly out of breath, but he could tell Cradie was in a hurry. He threw off the blanket. Then he quickly placed a halter over each of the unicorn's noses. Xander never led the unicorns anywhere. He let them do the walking. But that didn't mean he wanted any onlookers to get suspicions. They had to look like pets. Weird pets, yes. But pets nonetheless.

"So where to now?" Xander asked.

Cradie shrugged in the way that only four-legged unicorns can shrug. Now that they were here, she had no idea what was the next step. Her dream had been the furthest thing from clear.

"OK," whispered Blep, keeping his voice low so as not to attract any attention. The street was empty at the moment, but that didn't mean that someone couldn't be listening from a nearby window or shopfront. "Think. In your dream or nightmare or whatever. What else did Stalor say?"

"Nothing," whispered Cradie. "Just that there's a tonne of pickles."

Cradie began to walk as Ronk and Blep followed close behind. Xander held their lead loosely, not wanting to accidentally tug his friends the wrong way. He followed along, still attempting to get his breath.

"If this is the real deal," whispered Blep, "if this is one of them vision quests or something, then there's something you're missing."

"He just talked about pickles," Cradie answered. She thought about the gleam in Stalor's smile. She thought about his beautiful bright eyes. But she kept those parts to herself. "And he said they're green."

"RONK," brayed Ronk.

It wasn't a whisper. Ronk didn't know how to whisper. It was like he only had one volume setting, and it was stuck as loud as his system could go.

"Well yeah, obviously pickles are green," whispered Blep. "That's not gonna help us with–"

Blep felt a tug at his reins. He wasn't a fan of the feeling. He was about to tell Xander as much when he glanced back at the small boy with his now sweaty brown hair.

But Xander was pointing to a building beside them. He wasn't saying anything, except for an occasional huff or a puff.

"Gre-eee-eeeeeen," Cradie said. Blep looked at the sign on the building. It read: The Law Offices of Green & Green.

"Whattaya know. I stand corrected," Blep said. Then he walked towards the building's front door.

CHAPTER SEVEN

As is usually the case when faced with a door that needs to be opened, the front door to the Law Offices of Green & Green was locked tight. Xander put his hands on either side of his eyes and peered inside. If he had to guess, he would estimate that the last time Green & Green used this particular office, they drove a horse and cart to work.

The inside of the small room was covered in dust, and that was it. There was no desk, no computer, no phone. There wasn't even an overturned bin in the corner or a family of squirrels squatting rent-free. The place was completely empty, except for a ratty carpet with several snags.

"So we break in," Blep said.

"Shh!" Xander said, reminding Blep that Rainbow-Barfing Unicorns needed to keep secret the fact that they can indeed talk.

"Yeah, yeah," Blep whispered.

"We're not going to just start breaking and entering whenever you guys have weird dreams," said Xander.

It was a logical statement and one the Rainbow-Barfing Unicorns would probably have agreed with on any other occasion.

But on this day, Ronk was already standing inside the building.

"How did he–?" Xander started to say as Ronk used his front hoof to unlock the door.

"RONK!" Ronk said as Blep and Cradie strolled inside the building.

"He went around the back," said Cradie, as if she understood this particular "ronk" well enough to translate.

Xander looked both ways to make sure no one was watching. Then he, too, entered the Law Offices of Green & Green.

As usual, Cradie led the way. She trotted quickly through the front room and down the corridor that led to the back. At the end of the corridor, she could see the back door, still open from when Ronk had entered. But to the right, there was another set of doors. The first led to a small bathroom. The second door was shut. Cradie nudged the handle with her horn. It popped open. The door creaked loudly as Cradie stood in place in the corridor.

The room inside was as empty as the one near the front door. A dusty hardwood floor lined cracked walls and a window that had been boarded up. But none of that mattered. In the centre of the wall, Cradie found what she was looking for. A bright purple and white circle swirled impossibly, just off the floor. Grape-smelling light poured into the room and filled Cradie's nostrils.

"Whoa," said Xander. He had finally caught his breath, but was in the process of losing it again. This portal was just that impressive. "OK," he said. "We need to think this through and not make any rash decisions or–"

Cradie usually wouldn't have interrupted, but she was already in the process of making one of those rash decisions. She ran full speed at the portal and then leaped through. Her reins trailed after her.

"Or we could do just the opposite of what I was saying," said Xander. He watched as Blep and Ronk followed their leader.

"We're totally going to miss today's performance," Xander said. And then he stepped through the swirling mass of light as well.

CHAPTER EIGHT

"AHHHHHH!!!!!!" was all Xander could manage to say.

To be fair, it conveyed his thoughts pretty accurately. He was falling through the air at the moment. If he had been in his right mind, he would have worked out how far he was falling. But he was in anything but his right mind.

To his credit, he stopped screaming about twenty seconds after he landed.

It took Xander a few moments to take in his surroundings. He had fallen into a massive leaf pile. Red, green and yellow leaves were swirling in the air around him in all directions. They blocked his vision. But he didn't complain. If not for the leaf pile breaking his fall, he would probably have broken something far worse.

When the leaves and Xander's heartbeat both settled down, he could finally see his surroundings. The forest didn't look too different from the woods that occupied the mountain behind his house. The leaves were the same colours he was used to. As was the blue sky and the green grass. For another dimension, this world was suspiciously like Earth.

And then all of the sudden, it wasn't.

"Shhh," said a whispered voice coming from the tree line.

Xander strained to see the source of the noise. A shape stood draped in shadows. But the shape was all wrong. It wasn't a human, and it wasn't a unicorn, either. It looked like someone wearing a costume, the kind you would see a mascot wearing at a football match, or someone sweating inside at an amusement park.

"Hello?" Xander said. He was just now realizing that the Rainbow-Barfing Unicorns were nowhere in sight.

"Shhh!" the voice whispered. It sounded harsher this time.

"I'm Xander," Xander said. "Who . . . who are you?"

"SHHHHHHH!!!!" the voice responded. It was even louder. It was louder than Xander, in fact.

Xander thought that defeated the purpose of shushing someone, but he didn't say anything.

For the moment at least, he was quite willing to follow orders.

The figure took a few steps forward. The light breaking through the trees landed directly on its weird head. Xander gasped. The creature looked like a cross between a mouse and a bear. The head looked mouse-like, but the body was all bear. It was a terrible combination, really. Xander wished it was the other way around. Mice-sized bears he could deal with.

"Can you speak English?" Xander asked. He whispered this time. The last thing he wanted to do was offend a mouse-bear.

"Shhh!" the creature scolded. It was a bit quieter now. The mouse-bear thing looked from side to side. It was as if it was worried about someone seeing him with a human.

Xander could see it better now as the creature

stepped even closer to him. Its brown fur shifted in the gentle breeze. Its pink tail curled around its body, stopping just in front of its lips.

The mouse-bear didn't hold its finger to its mouth when it shushed Xander. It preferred to use its tail instead. Xander studied the creature's face and then noticed something strange about it. Something strange other than the fact that it was a giant mouse-bear who shushed people, that is.

The weird beast was wearing a tiny hat. It looked like a miniature samurai helmet. The metal hat was barely bigger than Xander's fist. The small little thing looked odd on the giant animal's head. Its red and gold colouring gleamed in the sunlight.

Xander was so focused on the tiny hat that he didn't see the mouse-bear reaching towards him. By the time he noticed the massive paw moving

towards his head, it was too late. There was nothing Xander could do. The mouse-bear did exactly what he wanted.

He placed another tiny hat on Xander's head.

CHAPTER NINE

Would you kindly keep your voice down? the mouse-bear said. But his mouth didn't move. He didn't make a sound. No, he wasn't talking at all. He was thinking at Xander.

"What?" Xander said.

Stop talking! thought the mouse-bear. *All you have to do is think!*

Weird, thought Xander.

The mouse-bear nodded his head. He actually heard Xander's thoughts.

To your people, it might seem odd, thought the mouse-bear. *But to mine, this is how we communicate here.*

By telepathy? Xander thought.

You could call it that, yes, thought the mouse-bear. *My name is Tobias.*

Oh, thought Xander. *I'm Xander. Nice to meet you.* Xander wasn't quite getting the hang of this whole talking without talking thing. He suddenly realized that Tobias had access to his brain. What if he thought the wrong thing?

Don't think anything embarrassing, Xander thought to himself. *Don't think about the time you forgot to wear underwear to school.*

Underwear? thought Tobias.

You heard that? thought Xander.

Very clearly, yes.

Oh, man, Xander thought. His cheeks turned bright red.

Think nothing of it, thought Tobias. *I don't quite understand human undergarments. As you can see, we Mear wear fur instead of your . . . clothing.*

Mear?

We're not called mouse-bears.

What? Xander thought.

You're thinking that right now, Xander. You're calling me a mouse-bear with your mind. That's quite an offensive term.

Oh. Sorry, Xander thought.

The proper term is Mear, thought the Mear.

Mear.

Yes.

Um, Mr Mear . . . Xander began to think.

Tobias is fine.

Um, Mr Tobias . . . thought Xander.

Just Tobias, Xander. I can read your thoughts. We've just met, but we're closer than you can imagine.

Oh, thought Xander.

This was starting to creep him out. He adjusted the tiny hat on his head. He realized that he was only hearing Tobias due to this little metal device, but even that thought wasn't comforting. And why did the hat have to be so small? It looked like something a tiny teddy bear would wear.

The term Teddy Bear is offensive to my people, too, thought Tobias.

I didn't know you were listening, Xander thought.

You're wondering where your friends are, aren't you?

Yes, thought Xander. He was indeed wondering that very thing.

Well, I have good news and bad news on that subject, thought Tobias. He sat down on a nearby fallen tree. He wanted to look Xander right in the eyes for this conversation. Towering over him simply would not be the proper etiquette.

What's the bad news? Xander asked. He could smell the Mear's breath. It smelled of fish and blueberries.

Your friends have been taken by the police.

Xander was stunned. *There are police mouse-bears?*

Mears, Tobias corrected with a sigh.

What's the good news? asked Xander.

We have about a minute until the police arrive here once more.

That's good news? Xander thought.

Well, thought Tobias, *it is if we start running. Right. Now.*

CHAPTER TEN

As they ran through the woods, Xander learned all about the strange world he was accidentally exploring. Luckily, thoughts don't get winded. Even when sprinting at full speed, thoughts come out quite loudly. They might be a bit jumbled due to all the chaos, but they could be heard by others very easily. Or they could be heard by others wearing a ridiculous tiny metal hat, at least.

This world was called Shushyerbum. It was a place of quiet and serenity. To speak out loud was not just considered rude, it was against the law.

When the Rainbow-Barfing Unicorns had arrived, Blep had done his usual complaining. Cradie had done her usual leading and Ronk had done his usual ronking. All of it was out loud. It didn't take long for the police Mears to catch up with them. Tobias had watched from a nearby blueberry bush. He had seen the whole thing happen as he ate his afternoon snack.

Without tiny hats of their own, the Rainbow-Barfing Unicorns had no idea that they were doing anything wrong. The police weren't about to tell them and risk getting thrown in prison themselves. So they had rounded up Xander's friends and marched them down to the prison caves at the far end of this wooded island.

By the time Tobias had finished thinking all this information to Xander, the two of them had reached a steep drop off. Tobias had been down on all fours for their run. And with a nod of his head, he thought, *Hop on my back, Xander.*

Xander did as he was told. He was doing his best to pant without making a sound. It took all of his concentration just to do that. He would welcome a free ride at this point.

Holding onto the fur around Tobias's neck, Xander felt his body lurch forwards. Tobias had leaped off the cliff. Xander wanted to scream, but he kept the screaming to his thoughts.

You even think loud, thought Tobias as he landed on a small dirt ledge.

The leap had been graceful. For all his size, Tobias was quite agile. He had made this jump thousands of times, and it showed.

Tobias balanced on the ledge. He walked slowly but surely for a little way. The ledge was less than a metre wide. Xander wasn't sure how a Mear Tobias's size could even fit on it, let alone walk. But Tobias managed just the same.

I hope you realize, I'm not a large Mear, Tobias thought.

Oh, I . . ., Xander began to think.

I'm quite average for my age and height, thought Tobias. *I'm not fat, if that's what you're thinking.*

I wasn't thinking that.

I can hear your thoughts, Xander, Tobias thought.

I . . . I wasn't thinking that . . . on purpose?

Hmph, Tobias thought.

After a few more dangerous steps, Tobias rounded a corner. Xander felt a wet mist on his face. A waterfall stood before him. It was massive. Its water cascaded down the side of the cliff, opening up to a small pond and a creek below. The cliffs lined each side of this valley. It was like a hidden oasis in an already fertile forest.

Welcome to my home, thought Tobias. Then he jumped off the ledge entirely.

CHAPTER ELEVEN

Blep didn't like the tiny hat the police Mears had placed on his head. It was a green and yellow beanie, complete with a tiny fake helicopter blade. The whole thing was made out of metal, and it was much too small. He felt ridiculous wearing it. It didn't help that Ronk kept looking at him and laughing.

It's not like Ronk's hat was much better. The little metal top hat wasn't fooling anyone into thinking that Ronk was a posh gentleman.

Cradie's hat was much more befitting of her character. It was a beret-like cap, also made of metal. It didn't look comfortable, but she wore it well. Blep thought Cradie wore most things well.

Thanks, Cradie thought at him.

Blep had forgotten that she could hear his thoughts now. He blushed. Fortunately, he was red, so it didn't show . . . much.

As I was thinking, thought the Mear chief of police standing in front of them. *It is quite illegal to speak words here in Shushyerbum.*

But we didn't know the rules when we got here, thought Cradie.

Ignorance of the law does not make one above the law, thought the police chief.

The chief was a small Mear, as Mears go. He stood only a bit taller than the Rainbow-Barfing Unicorns, who themselves were smaller than most miniature ponies. The police chief's black fur was shiny. He was used to presenting a professional image. He was a very serious Mear, despite the tiny metal police hat he wore on his head. He was a very serious Mear, indeed.

But we . . . , Cradie began to think. Before she could think any further, the chief of police interrupted her.

The door, Bartholomew, he thought.

If the police chief was small, Bartholomew was his equal and opposite. He was a massive Mear. He towered over the Rainbow-Barfing Unicorns, as well as the other police Mears behind him. However, his metal police hat was the same size as the chief's.

Bartholomew stepped forward and flung shut a door made of iron bars. It came to a clanking halt when it hit the other side of the cave wall. Cradie examined the door. It wasn't rectangular at all. It matched the shape of the opening of the cave they were standing in.

Their cave was just one of many on the cliff side. It seemed that the Mear police had plenty of prisoners. Talking was a hard habit to break. Especially for those from other worlds.

You ought to be happy there, at least, thought the police chief. *All of you together like that. You really should be thanking me.*

Cradie looked at the police chief. She was confused. What would she possibly thank this Mear for?

What's he talking about? thought Blep.

Thinking about, corrected a thought from behind the Rainbow-Barfing Unicorns. There was a figure standing at the back of the cavern. His thoughts were instantly familiar.

It's you, thought Cradie.

That's right, darling, thought the voice. *Police Chief Regis was referring to me.*

Stalor stepped out of the shadows. Cradie tried to keep her ecstatic thoughts to herself. She did a terrible job of it.

CHAPTER TWELVE

Good to see you all again, thought Stalor.

Cradie rushed over to her friend and gave him a big hug. It was as big a hug as a unicorn could muster.

Blep eyed Stalor from across the prison cell. He did his best to hunt for flaws in the handsome stallion. He wasn't making any progress on that front. Even the tiny metal fedora Stalor wore on his head looked cool. It tilted in just the right way.

Stalor was the only unicorn who could go through a zombie transformation and still look as perfect as ever. If his skin was dry, you couldn't tell due to its colouring. His eyes didn't look nasty or creepy. His teeth remained in perfect shape.

He hadn't even bothered to change his name like the rest of them. Why would he?

Thanks for the kind words, Stalor thought
to Blep.

Blep's eyes went wide. He had forgotten about
the whole mind reading thing again. Now he was
only helping to swell Stalor's already inflated ego.

Stalor smiled his million-dollar smile at Blep.
Blep returned a sarcastic expression.

Then Stalor turned his attention to Cradie. *Did
you come here – all the way to Shushyerbum – for me?*
he asked her.

Of course, Cradie thought. *We couldn't just
abandon you.*

So you heard my thoughts from your world?
Stalor thought.

Cradie was taken aback for a second. *Your
thoughts? You mean the dreams?*

*Is that how you heard me? I kept thinking to you
as hard as I could. I wasn't sure if my thoughts would*

reach you in your dimension. *Especially as you didn't have one of these tiny hat receivers.*

They did reach me! thought Cradie in an excited tone. She was a bit embarrassed about how excited she sounded. *My dreams kept getting interrupted with the words "pickle" and "tonne". It was Xander who worked out that you were saying "Pickletown."*

I knew we had a . . . special connection, Stalor thought.

Oh, please, Blep thought. This time he didn't care who heard him.

The guards had spoken about a portal to this realm, one that led to the world of the humans, Stalor thought. *It was my hope that you had been banished to that world. That you would learn of this Pickletown as I had.*

I did! Cradie thought. *It all worked!*

Yeah, it worked great, thought Blep. *Look where it got us.*

Yes, thought Stalor. *I'm sorry about all of this. I wish it could have gone any other way.*

Sure ya are, thought Blep.

But I do have one question, thought Stalor. *Who is this . . . Xander you speak of?*

He's a human, thought Cradie. *A friend of ours.*

So humans really do exist? thought Stalor.

They're real, thought Cradie. *They're all over Earth. That's what they call the world we were sent to.*

And he came here with you? To Shushyerbum?

We thought he did, thought Cradie. *But he must have come through later. After the police rounded us up. Time can be wonky in those portals.*

Well, thought Stalor. *I don't know what time it is on your Earth right now, but in this world, it's getting late. And you've been through so much.*

I do feel exhausted, thought Cradie. She looked out of the prison cell. Sometime during their conversation, the sun had set. The last hints of daylight were barely lingering outside the bars of the cave.

I think our best bet is to get some sleep and regroup in the morning, thought Stalor.

You're right, thought Cradie. *Let's get some sleep guys,* she thought as she looked at Ronk and Blep. *We'll work this out tomorrow.*

Blep reluctantly agreed. He and Ronk laid down near the bars, while Cradie took a position a bit closer to Stalor. Now that she had found him, she didn't want to let him out of her sight. Blep wanted to think something to her, but he didn't. Instead, he watched Cradie sleep until his own eyelids became heavy.

Then Blep, too, drifted away from the reality of Shushyerbum, and into another weird place. It was a dimension of dreams of Pegasia, of a world outside a locked cage.

CHAPTER THIRTEEN

Xander was growing impatient. To him,
it seemed to take forever for the sun to set in
Shushyerbum. And now that it had set, it took
another forever for the sky to fade to black.

As much as he was impressed by Tobias's
home in the valley near the waterfall, he was
ready to go and rescue his friends. He had never
felt so worried in his life. This was worse than
the time he'd completely forgotten to hand in his

book report at school. And something far worse than getting an F awaited Cradie, Blep and Ronk.

I think we can go soon, thought Tobias as he walked over towards the rock Xander had been sitting on for the last twenty minutes. The pair had long since dried off after landing in the large pool of water at the bottom of the cliff. Even Tobias's fur showed no signs of moisture.

Good, thought Xander. He was ready to head to the prison Tobias had told him about. But he had no idea how to get his friends out once he got there.

We'll work out a way, Xander, thought Tobias.

Xander hadn't been guarding his thoughts closely enough. Tobias could hear his jumbled notions of worry and panic.

But before we go, I need to show you something of the utmost importance.

Um . . . OK? Xander was confused.

Follow me, thought Tobias. He led Xander down past the pond at the base of the waterfall and into a small cave. Tobias's massive form seemed to barely squeeze inside the cavern's opening. Xander didn't have quite the same problem as he followed him.

Xander continued with Tobias through the cave. His eyes adjusted to his darker surroundings fairly quickly. But when they turned a corner, Xander's eyes needed to adjust once again. There swirling in front of him was a white and purple portal of light. If it wasn't so bright, it could have been mistaken for a huge lollipop.

You have another portal? Xander thought.

I do. Most portals are one way as you're probably aware. I'm the only one who knows about this one. It's secure. It will get you back to your town of pickles.

Xander smiled. *Thanks, but . . . but . . . why are you helping us, Tobias? I don't understand any of this.*

There's more going on here than you realize, thought Tobias. *My people have been trying to trick Earthlings into our world for decades. But the portal you used? It's been inactive for as long as I've been aware of it. Humans just don't come here any more.*

Why not? Xander asked with his thoughts. *And why do you guys want us here anyway? One thing about my people, we're certainly not quiet.*

Oh, I don't want you here, thought Tobias. *But I'm in the minority, I suppose. I want to help get you home.*

But why? Xander asked.

Isn't it obvious, thought Tobias. *I'm a vegetarian. Unlike the rest of the Mears, I don't eat humans.*

CHAPTER FOURTEEN

There. Can you see them? thought Tobias.

I can't even see you, thought Xander in response. He was being honest. There he was, hiding behind some bushes near the prison. But it was so dark he had trouble seeing at all.

Tobias had climbed a nearby tree to get a better view of the prison and had disappeared in the process. If this world had a moon, it certainly wasn't out tonight. There was a lamp post near the cells, but the bush in front of Xander was blocking it. He was going to need a better view.

Xander took a breath and shut his eyes. Ever since Tobias had mentioned that Mears not only enjoyed eating humans, but considered them a delicacy, he was having a tough time being brave. They hadn't passed any Mears on the way to the centre of town, but he didn't want to ruin that winning streak now by getting spotted.

You can do this, Xander, thought Tobias. His thoughts seemed whispered. It was as if he was directing them just to Xander so no one else could possibly overhear them.

Xander didn't respond. He opened his eyes and rushed towards a hedge closer to the caves. Once he was there, he could finally see the prison.

The prison was impressive to say the least. Who but mouse-bears would ever consider placing inmates in a natural prison? All they needed to do was add a set of iron bars, and their enemies stood no chance of burrowing through the solid rock of the cliff.

It was elegant in its simplicity, even if it did look a bit cold in those cells. Xander guessed that the Mears didn't worry about cold much. Their fur took care of that little detail.

The lamp post near the cells was just bright enough. Xander could make out a lone police Mear. Surprisingly, there were no other Mears in sight. This particular Mear was near one cell in particular.

As Xander's eyes adjusted, he could see that the Mear was talking to – or thinking to, rather – a prisoner. He strained to get a better look.

The figure on the other side of the bars was dark, but Xander could detect its shape. It was most certainly a unicorn!

Do you know that creature? thought Tobias quietly.

He's a unicorn, thought Xander. *But he's not one of my friends.*

The one you were looking for then?

Yeah, thought Xander. *That must be Stalor. I . . . I can't hear what he's . . . thinking.*

I don't think that matters, thought Tobias. *Look.*

Xander did as instructed. Tobias hadn't steered him wrong yet. The police Mear was lifting his tiny police hat off of his head. Underneath it was a set of keys. He inspected them, and then placed one key into the lock on the prison cell door. He opened the door, just a little bit.

And then the Mear turned and walked away.

Looks like you're not the only vegetarian in Shushyerbum, thought Xander.

It would appear I am not, thought Tobias.

CHAPTER FIFTEEN

Where are we going? Cradie thought. She was trying to keep her thoughts quiet but was not successful.

This was a crazy situation. They were running through the woods of another dimension, escaping from police officers who were half bear and half mouse. It wasn't exactly easy to remain calm.

Anywhere other than here, thought Stalor. Then he added, *To your friend, hopefully.*

Our friend? Cradie thought.

You said there was a human? Xander? Do you have any idea where he would be?

No! yelled Cradie in her mind. *He could still be on Earth, staring at the portal for all I know!*

If this is going to work, thought Stalor, *he needs to be here.* He stopped and looked at Cradie directly in the eyes. *Tell me he's here, Cradie.*

I'm here, Xander thought. He was huffing and puffing again, but his mind wasn't. His thoughts came across clear as day.

Cradie and Blep looked across the woods to see Xander and Tobias. They smiled. Behind them, Ronk wasn't smiling. It was odd behaviour for the unicorn. He nearly always greeted Xander by attempting to leap into his arms, an action that almost never worked out well for either party. Cradie thought that maybe Ronk was just starting to work that out.

Xander! Cradie's thoughts exclaimed. *You won't believe what happened!*

We saw everything, thought Xander.

You did? asked Stalor.

We were near the hedge, thought Xander. *We couldn't hear you, but we saw that police officer let you out of the cell.*

Wait, thought Cradie. *What? You woke me up and told me you'd picked the lock.*

Stalor smiled at the faded purple unicorn. It was dark under the canopy of trees, but Cradie could certainly see his perfectly white set of teeth.

Sorry, Stalor thought. *I was just trying to impress you, I suppose. I bribed a guard with some Mear money I had stashed away. That was it.*

Heroic, Blep thought in a sarcastic voice.

Who is your friend? Stalor asked with his mind, nodding towards Tobias.

But before Xander could respond, Ronk ran into the centre of the group. His face looked panicked.

Ronk, what's–

We need to get out of here, Ronk thought.

For the first time since they had left Pegasia, the Rainbow-Barfing Unicorns were actually hearing Ronk's real voice. And it was saying more than just, **"RONK."**

How are you– Cradie tried to think before Ronk interrupted.

I heard Stalor. He thought I was sleeping, or just didn't think I understood. But we're in big trouble. They're following us. The Mears. They'll be here any minute.

Now, Ronk, I don't know what you think you heard– began Stalor.

You told that officer you'd lead him to Xander! I heard you! Ronk thought. His brow was furrowed. Cradie couldn't remember seeing him that angry before. *Stalor traded his own freedom in exchange for Xander's life.*

Why would he do that? Cradie thought.

Because Mears eat humans, thought Tobias. *Well, other Mears, I mean.*

Yes, thought a strange voice from the shadows behind the group. *Yes we do.*

CHAPTER SIXTEEN

Thank you for your fine work, Stalor, thought Police Chief Regis as he walked closer to Xander and the Rainbow-Barfing Unicorns. Behind him, two other Mears followed him into view. They were the largest Mears the Rainbow-Barfing Unicorns had seen yet.

You really did this, Cradie thought. She wasn't

asking a question. She was working everything out now. *The dreams, calling us here, it was all to save your own skin.*

That's not true, thought Stalor.

"Just talk already," said Blep. "What's the worst they're gonna do to us now? Lock us up again?"

"I didn't think about . . . about trading you for my freedom," said Stalor. He was following Blep's lead and actually talking out loud. "Not until you mentioned Xander. But I'm sure they won't hold you. Not when you hand over your human. We can all leave here together. They don't want unicorns."

Please, thought Police Chief Regis, *keep your voices down.*

"You've got us shakin' in our hooves over here," Blep said to him in his usual joking voice.

The faded red unicorn just didn't care about the rules of Shushyerbum any more.

"You want us to trade our friend for our freedom?" Cradie said. She was appalled.

"Well, yes," said Stalor, "I mean, it's not like he's a unicorn. He's not like us."

"Nor is he a monster!" shouted Tobias as he leaped onto Stalor.

The handsome unicorn fell backwards into Chief Regis and his Mear officers. Despite their size, the two large Mears buckled under the impact and fell directly on top of their chief.

"Run!" shouted Tobias.

While the others escaped, Tobias did his best to stay on top of Stalor. His furry back smooshed the unicorn's face into the dirt. "Boy, it's fun to talk," said Tobias. "Talk, talk, talk. I've really missed this."

Despite the darkness of the woods, Xander remembered the way. There was a partially worn trail through the woods. He just had to stay on course.

Cradie galloped after her human friend. Blep and Ronk followed. Even though she wanted to, Cradie didn't look back. She cared about Stalor, but she couldn't bear to look at him at the moment, no pun intended. She doubted she could ever look at Stalor the same way again.

Less than five minutes later, Xander stopped at the edge of a cliff. "We've got to get down there!" he said, pointing to a thin ledge below.

Blep nodded. He was willing to be the group's guinea pig. Someone had to go first. So he leaped.

His hooves landed on the thin ledge. Dust and dirt slid out beneath him. But he kept his balance. He looked back up.

"OK!" he called. "It's OK!"

Ronk was next. He was hardly graceful, but he managed. Cradie followed. She had an easier time of it than her friends.

"Go without me!" Xander called. "The ledge is too narrow! I can't make it on my–"

"Come on now," said Tobias from behind Xander. "No need to give up the ghost just yet." He nodded towards his back, and Xander jumped aboard. Tobias leaped through the air and once again landed perfectly on the narrow ledge. "Shall we?" he said.

CHAPTER SEVENTEEN

The white and purple portal of pure light swirled in front of them.

"It's beautiful," said Cradie. She looked over at Xander. He was still dripping water onto the cave floor. They all were. But as usual, Xander looked the silliest.

"You first," Cradie said.

As the only person in the cavern on the Mears' menu, Xander didn't argue. He stepped through the portal and disappeared from sight.

Ronk followed, and then Blep after him.

"You're coming with us," Cradie said to the large Mear standing next to her.

"No," said Tobias. "I'm afraid I must remain here, in hiding. It is my sworn duty to guard this precious portal in case any other Mears attempt to follow you."

"They won't," said Stalor. Tobias turned around and saw the dark unicorn standing behind him. "I'll make sure of it."

Stalor took a few steps back. Then he ran directly at Cradie. She was too surprised to react. She just shut her eyes and braced for impact. Tobias was too slow to do anything, either. Stalor's sharp horn neared Cradie.

Then Stalor turned away at the last second. He struck the cave wall next to her. The wall rumbled, just slightly. A few rocks dislodged from above and rolled down the wall. Stalor backed up again.

"What are you doing?" Cradie asked.

"Fixing my mess," said Stalor. Then he charged the wall again and collided with it. More rocks and dirt began to shake loose.

"Don't," Cradie said. "Please . . ."

"You better get going," said Stalor as he charged the wall again. He flashed Cradie his famous smile. "The Mears are right behind me. And this cave isn't going to be standing for long."

Tobias turned to Cradie. He picked her up and threw her through the portal.

He nodded at Stalor, but the unicorn didn't see him. He was charging the wall again.

Tobias stepped through the portal. When he looked over his large, furry shoulder, all he could see were rocks collapsing in front of the portal. Stalor was nowhere to be seen. Everything was just dust and rubble.

CHAPTER EIGHTEEN

"We've got to go back," Cradie said as soon as she got to her hooves.

The Rainbow-Barfing Unicorns were standing in a car park now. It was behind Pickletown's only supermarket. Judging by the number of potholes and weeds sprouting up through those potholes, it didn't look like this particular car park got any use these days.

The Rainbow-Barfing Unicorns had fallen out of the sky just above the car park before their portal had swirled out of sight.

The fall was enough to wind them. Xander
had even scraped his knee in the process.

"He closed the portal behind us," said Tobias.
"You can go back the way you arrived, but if
you do, Shushyerbum will be your new and
permanent home."

"No!" Cradie yelled.

"Cradie–" Blep began.

"Don't you say anything!" said Cradie. She
was angry. She seemed like she was mad at the
whole world. "You always hated him! You don't
care if Stalor is trapped there forever!"

Blep didn't answer. He didn't make a comment
or one of his jokes. Instead, he just walked over
to his friend. He put his front legs around Cradie,
and gave her a hug. It was awkward at first. Blep
wasn't sure he even remembered how to hug at
all. But he got the hang of it.

And soon, Cradie calmed down and hugged him back.

"Let's go home," said Xander.

Cradie tried to smile as she nodded. But a smile didn't come. No one expected it to.

CHAPTER NINETEEN

"You're sure you'll be fine up here?" Xander
said. He and Tobias stood in the clearing at the
top of the mountain behind his house. It was
a special place for all involved. This was where
Xander had first discovered the Rainbow-Barfing
Unicorns. Behind Tobias and Xander stood
Cradie, Ronk and Blep.

Tobias nodded. Then he turned his head a bit,
as if he was speaking. But he said nothing.

"Oh," Tobias said. "I keep forgetting. Our little
hats don't work on your world."

Tobias took off his samurai helmet and examined it. Then he placed it back on his head. He had grown quite fond of the tiny little device.

"Yeah," said Xander, looking back at Ronk.

Out of everyone, the hats had benefited Ronk the most. When he wore his, he could actually communicate. But Ronk just shrugged.

"RONK," Ronk said. Then he began munching on some grass. It was just another average day in the life of the strangest Rainbow-Barfing Unicorn.

"I'll come and visit as much as you want," said Xander. "There's a nice cave down on the east side of the mountain that I think you'll just love. It's really quiet."

"It will be fine, my little human friend," said Tobias. "But to be honest, the last thing I'm looking for is quiet at the moment."

Xander smiled and hugged the large

mouse-headed creature. Tobias wrapped his tail around Xander, hugging him back.

"This is sweet and everything, but can we go home now?" Blep said. "I'm hungry, and that rubbish ain't gonna eat itself."

"Oh now Mr Hugs-A-Lot can't handle a little emotion," Cradie teased. Blep blushed. This time, it was dark enough to show up on his cheeks.

"Gimme a break," he said.

Cradie smiled, and gave her friend a quick peck on the cheek. Blep blushed an even deeper shade of red. For a brief second, he looked just as rosy as his old Raspberry Jelly self.

Xander waved goodbye to Tobias and set off down the mountain. The Rainbow-Barfing Unicorns followed, with Ronk taking up the rear.

"RONK!" Ronk brayed. With that, a beautiful rainbow decorated the sky, lighting their way back home.

CHARACTER SPOTLIGHT:
STALOR!

Height: 1 metre, 80 centimetres

Horn length: 25 centimetres

Weight (before barfing): 195 pounds

Weight (after barfing): 194 pounds

Colour: teal

Barf colour: full spectrum

This once-missing zombie unicorn is
by far the handsomest of all Rainbow-
Barfing Unicorns. Stalor also seems
unbelievably valiant and heroic. That
is, until you get to know him better . . .
(Thus, the "unbelievable" part.)

GLOSSARY

banish send someone away from a place and order them not to return

bray make a sound like the call of a donkey

dimension place in space and time

expression look on someone's face

portal door or passage to another place

spectrum range of colours shown when light shines through water or a prism

BARF WORDS

blow chunks barf

heave barf

hork barf

hurl barf

puke barf

ralph barf

regurgitate barf

retch barf

spew barf

throw up barf

upchuck barf

vomit barf

yak barf

JOKES!!

What type of Rainbow-Barfing Unicorns only go out at night?

Night-mares!

What do you give a sick Rainbow-Barfing Unicorn?

Cough stirrup!

What type of Rainbow-Barfing Unicorn can jump higher than a car?

All of them! Cars can't jump.

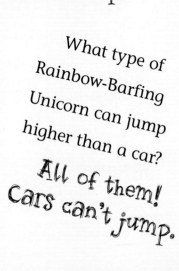

Why did Xander ride the Rainbow-Barfing Unicorn?

He was too heavy to carry.

What's a Rainbow-Barfing Unicorn's favourite sport?

Stable tennis.

Why did the Rainbow-Barfing Unicorn eat with its mouth open?

It had bad stable manners!

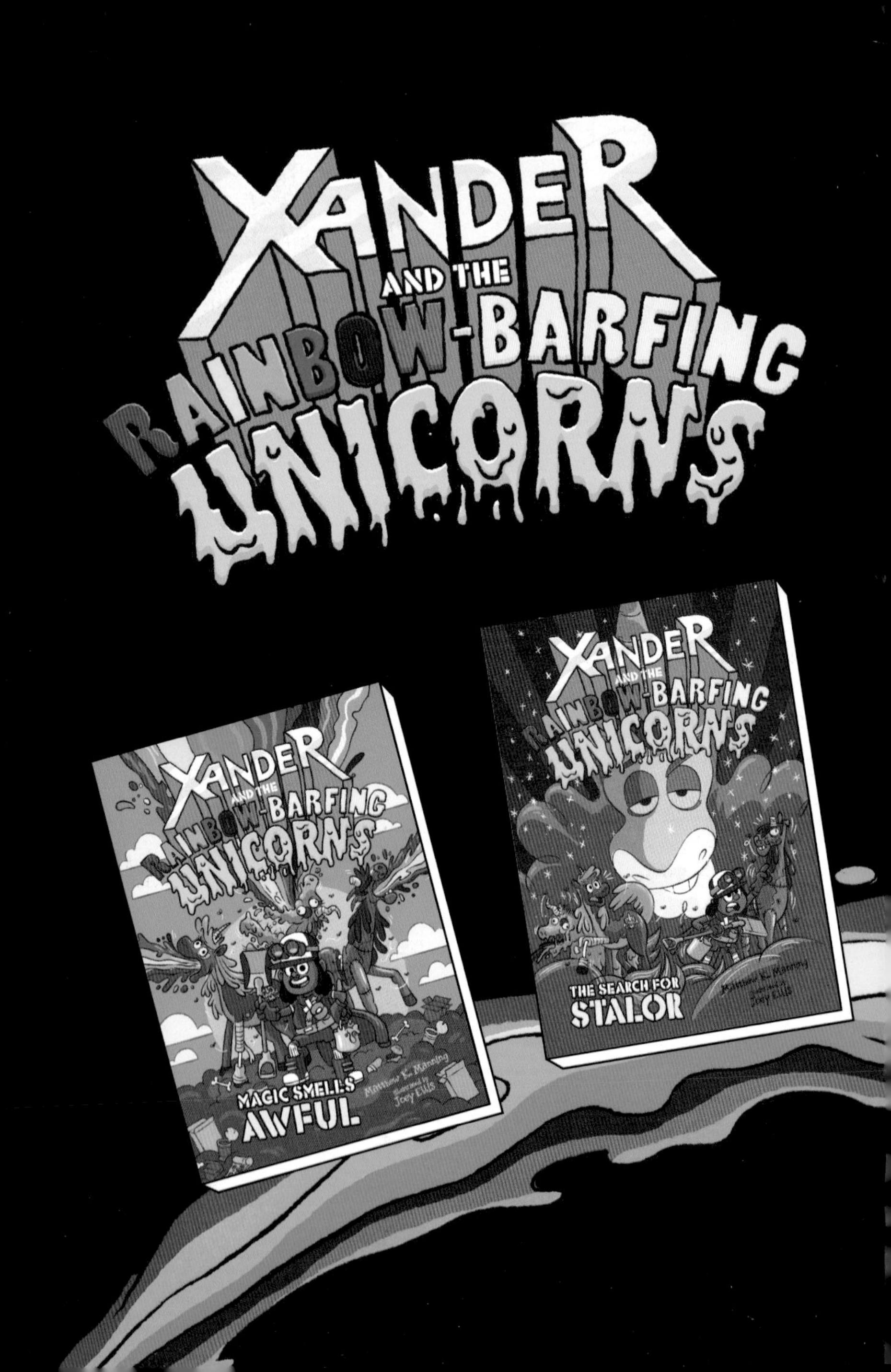
XANDER AND THE RAINBOW-BARFING UNICORNS
XANDER AND THE RAINBOW-BARFING UNICORNS
MAGIC SMELLS AWFUL
Matthew K. Manning
Joey Ellis
XANDER AND THE RAINBOW-BARFING UNICORNS
THE SEARCH FOR STALOR
Joey Ellis

READ THEM ALL!

raintree

a Capstone company — publishers for children

AUTHOR

The author of more than seventy-five books, Matthew K. Manning has written several comic books as well, including the hit *Batman/ Teenage Mutant Ninja Turtles Adventures* miniseries. Currently the writer of the new IDW comic book series *Rise of the Teenage Mutant Ninja Turtles*, Manning has also written comics starring Batman, Wonder Woman, Spider-Man, the Justice League, the Looney Tunes and Scooby-Doo. He currently lives in North Carolina, USA, with his wife, Dorothy, and their two daughters, Lillian and Gwendolyn.

ILLUSTRATOR

Joey Ellis lives and works in North Carolina, USA, with his wife, Erin, and two sons. Joey writes and draws for books, magazines, comics, games, big companies, small companies and everything else in between.